Savior

Season one:

Darkheart

Book Two:

Under The Weight of a Spirit

The writer:

Amin Ebrahimi

Contents at a glance

Under The Weight of a Spirit

Chapter I

The laboratory

A part of what have happened for me so far, I have narrated for Sayna. In Fact, which was a background to prepare her to confront what will be happen later. I think, passing of the past days may have acquired the needed condition, while I was replacing the stages, which she must pass to higher ones.

Therefore, today, she could enter to the new stage. I went to her room as every day. He was sitting in the Big Hall and speaking with lord Dracula, I can clearly see how the creatures of this collection have cope with her, while the linkage between then can be observed. Although, Lord Dracula has spoken a couple of words. However, he was speaking with sayna.

I tried to keep a smile on my face to start an enteric day.

"Are you ready for a new day? " I asked.

"Hello" She said while he noticed of me.

"Now we can leave." She said, while ending her speaking with lord Dracula.

We left the room walking in the corridor, "I hope you can remember the room, which seen several days ago, but we changed our decision of seeing if." I said.

"I can remember that room, which was like a lab. " Sayna said.

When we reached that room we entered going up the metal stairs arriving to the first port of the lab. In fact, it was a collection of tableaus and pictures, while installed on the wall. As well as a series of engineering instruments.

"today, you want to introduce the major of your education, I guess." As Sayna saw these instruments.

"no, however, I should remind you a brief explanation on this subject." I answered I continued, as I graduated I registered a company. I had decided to start constructing different buildings using the capital given by my family. Since, I counselled with my father's friend to get familiar with the introductions and principles, as well relevant activities.

Of his friend to cooperate in two the different project, which was operating in the town's hospital.

The first project includes repairing and reconstruction of the old building of hospital, while the second includes constructing the new building for the hospital, since. I don't know the place of operation in the first day, I went walking to the place accompanying the others. Different units of the hospital must be passed to arrive in the place of construction first.

No need to mention that we should keep the silence, passing these units as we did.

We passed different corridors and units. That was a big hospital having all the Unites which required in a comprehensive hospital.

As were reached the place of project operation, I noticed this place is complete isolated using plastic curtains to prevent entering dust to other units of the hospital.

Since, all personal of company was trying to make the least noise. Therefore, the overall project progresses slowly. Anyway the condition of project requires such work style and there was no replaceable way.

I showed Sayna a special that and mask to work. “These are the first mask and hat, I used in may works bringing me too much to memories ” I said.

I showed her a picture on the wall. “this picture is of those days.” I told her.

“is it that hospital?” Sayna asked.

“yes, exactly. Nevertheless, this is not the part, which we were working there. If you wolf to see that unit. You should look at the next picture.” I said.

“first day was completely spent on isolation of the new part by the construction group and preparing a plan how to conduct the project in the coming days, providing a list of needed instruments and tools. I continued.

The second day, I my set went to the workplace. Since, the corridors were similar to each other.

I walk to one this is a different corridor from the corridor I passed yesterday.

I wanted to ask one of the personal to guide me how to go the construction place, however, I didn’t know the name of work place from one hand. There were no medical tools in the place of our practice from the other hand. Therefore. I could not distinguish; which unit was our work place based in the medical tools! I had no way pass one corridor to the on other to find the project place. As I was passing the corridors to find the part, which the company was reconstructing it. I noticed the condition of a patient is not good in overall, while the physicians and nurses were standing around the patient trying to revive him. I stood at the door and looking at what was happening with no clear purpose. There was a mobile bed in that room, which used to transfer patient. However, the patient died as moving from the bed to the mobile bed. In the hands of hospital personals. His corpus transferred to the mobile bed and transferred to the other place. Seeing such situation occupied my mind for a while.

I have known before, the human includes not only the body, but also spirit. The spirit leaves the body of human, as dies. Therefore, this person who died in the hands of nurses has spirit in the first bed, while having no spirit in the mobile bed.

Was his weight same on the second bed comparing the first or different? This question was circling in my mind until found the place of operation finally.

The last sight of the patient does not leave me in the whole of way. The other workers of company asked me the reason of my lateness and I told them whole of story. I need much of time to think about if I find the answer of my questions.

I asked the agent manager of company to permit me not come to the work project for some days. They supposed seeing the death of that patient affects me negatively, they accepted. However, if they knew what I have on that cave, they would not even think of it!

I returned home starting to walk in its garden.

My mother saw my bad condition and got me close and asked me worriedly; "why you got home new, what happened? You have must been on you work project "

I told what happened, we were walking I noticed an old house closed to our house with no in habitants. I asked her about it and she said, this is a part of our house actually.

Your father decided to divide the house in to two part, which is empty and no one lives there.

“Is there anything in the house? ”I asked.

“I think there are the furniture and instruments of the ex-owner.” She answered. I asked her, shall I go there? She accepted and gave me the key of there. This was my first experience to have a separate place as a lab.

“did you change there to g lab?” Sayna asked.

“Yes. And this is the picture of there.” I answered.

“what a beautiful house.” she looked at the picture on the wall and said.

“of course, but its lab is more beautiful.” I answered.

I continued; that day I had a short looking at different parts of house. I changed the design of furniture is some parts. The cellar of the house was big and almost has no furniture.

The trees of house were untidy and the grasses were over – grown. I asked our gardener to cut them two days past and we could design the house as I desire. The noon of third day was rainy. I was standing in front of the window and writing a list of instruments I needed to buy. The rain stopped after a while, I got back our house considering what I want to do up to the late of night. It was morning and I should prepare to go to shop center. I was counting the seconds for the shop to be opened and I was the first, who entered, I selected, some office chairs and furniture, as well files to put the lab instruments and tools. In the sector of furniture. I paid the money and asked from the shopper to send them the old house, giving him the address. I went rapidly to another shop, which sells the lab instruments and tools.

I could buy another part of what I wanted, the third place, which I gone was the electrical instruments and chips and so on. The paid money shows preparing that lab brought me too much of cost.

I had a hard afternoon. There were too much of works to do. I should deliver what I have bought and guide the workers to put what they brought on their places. Since, a part of my buy–out came simultaneously. I had to move within the floors several times. The hardest stage was delivering and moving of a small oven of found workshop, all of bought tools and instruments were moved to the back yard and storage, which has been changed yard and storage. Which has been changed to a found workshop new, as all of. These works finished, it was almost night. I closed the door starting to work in the street. I sometime sat on the park chairs and watching those who were passing rapidly. I was looking on the houses, which have their own special story. I got home late night and slept soon. I got up at crock of down, I ate the breakfast on hurry and went to the old house, today, the agent of what I bought were supposed to come to install them and test the accurate performance of the instruments, as well giving a short brief introduction of how they work. Yesterday, a part of the instruments were installed in their places or files, except the small oven of metal melting, which has not been used. In contrast of the cellar, which has been changed to a furnished lab. The first floor still has kept the appearance of a residential house. I had bought some books with different subjects, that I postpone designing of them to the next day. I bought five computers.

Three of them were installed in the cellar for the experimental instruments, while the two remaining were installed in the library and the next room, titled as the, respectively in the archive room, except 3-dimensions printer, supposed to install in the corner of the cellar, while they were networked with the library computer.

The company, which sold the computer installed them is such way that can be used either separately or as a whole to bring a higher power, that was almost the last part of the lab establish meat, which has lasted several days, I went to the roof looking on the sky, then, I look at our house I noticed the party, which my mother was absence, I seized this time to conduct a part of my lab, since. I had no possibility to install a high antenna for now, I tried to use an old car parked in the yard as an antenna. I spent whole of the night, finally I could reach a desirable performance.

Now, the lab was ready. I could start an answer derived my question raised in the hospital.

Chapter II
The experience

As I got home, I was walking to my room, that I saw my parents sitting in the upper floor. I was happy to see them. I said hello and sat. My father asked me about the work, that I was during in the old house. As I told him, I'm working on a privet lab, he became very happy, but asked me to think more serious about working in the company of his friend, as well as distributing a time to come to the factory and working with him across my daily activities.

I appreciated his suggestion. That night spent only for speaking and chatting with them until midnight. The next morning, I was thinking what I can do to find an answer for my question? Maybe, the first stage is a tool to estimate the weight which must be also connected to the patient bed. I went to the old house and started to build a very sensitive digital scale, which could weight objects with a high accuracy, while can be self-arranged and self-calibrated regarding the environmental condition. I should consider a wireless part for this scale, which can send the information related weighting to the lab, in real time. In addition, a sector needed to be connected with the instruments, which control patient crucial signals, sending them to the lab. I designed these two circles had been before bought, some of them were supposed to be send. A whole day also spent on founding of some parts, which needed.

Then, I should assemble them needed several days to be fulfilled. I test them under different conditions. The received responses were ideal. I guessed building them in my lab needs several days. As building these instruments, I call for a company, which manufactures hospital beds and ordered 50 beds based on the desirable features. My order received within ten days, I put them in the back yard, occupying with installing of the two my hand made instruments on beds. I tested each of beds under different conditions to evaluate the accuracy of their performance. As building of the target beds finished, it was time of returning back to the hospital and preparing the required conditions to experiment. It was about one month, I have not been in the hospital so far. When I got hospital. The time of repairing there was almost finished and only one week was remained. That day, not only I was doing my work very well, but also I considering this case how to transfer the beds to hospital. The second day, I found out the hospital manager ordered some new tools and instruments for the recent repaired units. Besides, the, manufacture will deliver the items later due to increase of ordered items and I could replace my beds with ordered beds easily. therefore, I got the codes and got home adding a new part to all of the home adding a new part to all of the beds, this part was like a division box, working as an intermediate, which was an inter mediator between the instruments, which measure the patient crucial signals and the patient in such way that the measurement tools were not directly connected to the instrument first, they were connected to this division box, then,. They were connected to the patient crucial signals. In this way, all data of measurement tools obtained of patient general conditions, will be sent to these beds first. Then, they will be send to the lab.

Finally, they return back to the hospital monitor. A camera was installed on the on of new beds, which can be used to see the patient conditions or reading the tools connected to patient if necessary. In addition to a microphone to listen to the voice of nurses and physicians discussing about the patient. After installing these intermediators to the bed.

Now, this is time of changing the characteristics of hospital beds. First, I called to the manufactory of hospital beds and informed them of canceling my order, since, the company received so many of orders from side of the hospital. They accepted happily, provided that they have not been used. Tomorrow, the related expert of the company came to the old house and perceived the difference bill at the first sight. I explained him.

These are new exclusive beds of you company as he asked for the reason of the differences; while I was putting a picture of then in their catalogue in such way that he did not understand.

When he compared the beds with the models in his file, he was persuaded that there is no problem in the beds. He called to the manufacturing company and informed them of this fact that the beds not been used. They told him me can deliver the beds to the cargo to be send to another forget. I went upstairs and turned on my computer. Entering to order register system of that company was not so hard, however, there was a problem, the manufacturing company decided to send my beds to another city. This problem was also solved replacing the new order codes of hospital. I send new addresses to the cargo and came to the downstairs. I was waiting for the trucks from cargo. I accurately, focused on the address, which were given to the drivers of trucks, yes, they were right. That was the hospital of our city.

It seems changing of address was done accurately in the website of cargo. As the trucks delivered the beds, they went to the hospital. Tomorrow, I went to the hospital and I saw the new beds were brought to the recent repaired unit. The several ongoing days were spent on installing of beds by protocells, and technicians of the hospital, there for, I could supervise on the stages of instalment process, while controlling the performance of beds at the end. After completion of their installment. I only need to wait for opening of the new unit, during the remaining time for opening, I prepared fifty monitors and connected them to the center computer of lab, and so, o could easily observe all the hospitalized patients on the beds simultaneously.

In addition, the patient crucial signals were also shown on the monitors. all the results were saved on the central computer, while I could print them out to evaluate more, there was about one month until the commencing of the new project of company, which was a constructing the hospital new building. Fortunately, this period was enough for the experiments that I designed.

In the opening day, no patient was hospitalized in the repaired unit, was of all, twenty of the beds were transferred to another unit, and I did not know where they are. This worry was raising on me that what's happening may endanger the general procedure of my experience. Especially the transferred beds may not be used under the codes I designed. However, these twenty beds also send some data. Provided that they were in the hospital, and they could be useful. Therefore, if a human o these bed too, I could obtain the relevant data. This movement may be good. Why not! This subject inspired me to send some of the beds to baby unit.

I was in front of the thirty monitors waiting to hospitalize a patient on them.

First day, no one hospitalized in them, that was a good news that no one has not been needed to hospitalize in this unit from one side. However, that was not good for evaluating my experience, I only studied a book. Second day, the first patient was brought to this unit. An elderly women with a sort length. She was almost fat. Before, he was brought to this unit, I had seen her in a park closed to our house with several people of her age, while giving seeds to the birds. She had a good mood. She never considers herself as an elderly. She always passes a big part of park as she winding. I looked at the characteristics of patient registered on the hospital computer she is 89 years old. I titled her as number 1 n my lab characteristic system. "I hope she will be recovered. "I told myself.

I was continuously checking her crucial signals. I was looking at her face, while oxygen mask covered a considerable part of her face. She was calmly sleeping.

Studying the medical profile of her recovery.

The next day, another patient was brought to this unit. He was a young man injured due to a car accident, who was in comma. His aye was registered as 24. I have not seen him. I registered him as number 2 in my lab system. Too much of time has not been passed that the third patient is brought.

The third case was an offensive, who was shouted in on army fighting, his characteristics were registered as the number 3. Again, I started to evaluate these patients. The patient no.1 is an elderly women, who is slowly waiting for death.

The patient No.3 was a young man in comma who has no perception of his surrounded space.

Finally, the offensive man, who has race neither in this world nor the other for sure!

I was evaluating these three patients that the numbers fourth and fifth were brought.

The number four was a middle aged man, while the number fifth was a child, who was brought this unit due to severity of his illness and needed emergency cares.

As I completed the lab forms of these people felt tired and pained on my eyes, while it was night and I should come back to the house.

“if you tell me what is interesting in that old house, that you spend whole of your time there, it will make me happy, I think your family also is interested to see you among them “ my mother said.

“there is nothing interesting on that house, I’m only studying on a subject, which contributes my time a little more.” I laughed and told to my mother. ” Please, be careful not hurt yourself.” my mother said as she heard worriedly.

As I heard it I laughed, my mother called my father in the middle of my laughing as she herself was supervised.” do you hear our son is working on a new subject.” something that I don’t know what was it, tall down of my father’s hand.” yes I heard, god blesses both of us.” in this moment, Sayna while was listening to me said; “god bless them surly. I have not forgotten that day, however, this time … I don’t know.”

“It won't happen anymore. ”I laughed and told her.

I continued; I was watching the television and concerning that what will happen and what kind of result will be obtained.

Therefore, I went to bed to get up in the morning soon, to go to the old house. Tomorrow, I got up sooner. There were some work, which must be done, which took time and afternoon. As I was going to the old house, heard the horn of my mother's car asking me to get in her car. I told her I have some important works to do, however, she brought her head out of car window and said; "if you think your works are mere important than your mother's emotion, you can go."

As I heart it, I accepted and I got into her car. First, we returned to our house. I changed my clothes based on her taste. Then, both of us invited to a party of my mother's friend, who was invited, there were so many of people there. I don't them to me. However, I had a very bad feeling toward one middle aged man, who was trying to show himself as a gentleman.

Their party almost ended in the midnight and we got back home. I changed my clothes and left our house for the old one. I check the monitors. I count the number of patients.it seems five more patients were brought today. The monitor related to the offensive man started to send caution signals, seeming he is spending the last moments of his life I was accurately concerning the number of his weight to check, what happens. I was very eager to see experiment result. However, the revival team put a tool on the bed. That I has not measured it, as well the loads, which was creating due to the revival activity team leading this fact that weight estimation instruments were showing different numbers continuously. I should wait for finishing of their work to estimate an accurate weight. During their activity, I was noting the doe and value of medicines, which wore given or injected to minus it from patient weight finally. I needed too much of accuracy to do them exactly. Suddenly, I noticed the patient face on the monitor, which was being recorded through the camera on his head. As it was written about the background of this offensive man.

It was supposed he fears of nothing, however, his face completely sank in fear seeming he is confronting a terrible creature or his death was much horrible for then what he was supposed.

He had no power to move, only grabbing the bed by his hands. His sight was buying from the revival team to save him from death. This death, he was seeing a creator, while others were not. Seeming he is horribly teared and trying to refuge from that creature, in such way that, he had forgotten the wish of life. Nevertheless of all drudges, he died finally. I looked at the medicines were consumed during his hospitalization on that unit and revival condition. Regarding those medicines, the patient must not fell too much of pain as he was dying. Therefore, his grubbing on the bed blanched and some other stronger behavior of him must not be related to the pain, and can be guessed these behaviors were induced of something else, that he was confronting them on that moment. based on the information, which l have read about him, he was a felon man, may his sins led to his big fear as he was dying ? And questions like that. However, I was there concentrate on the registered weights, while misusing the current weight of patient from consumed medicines. However, it was more than the past. I look at the bed using remaining on the bed. It they remain on the bed, until transferring the patient number 3 to this bed, the measurement procedure would be disturbed.

A tittle tome was post and a hospital personnel come to bring them back. The camera of bed was showing the face of patient, while his eyes were open seeming he is not interested to leave this world, or he does not dare to close his eyes due to what he saw. Evaluating the data obtained the patient number 3 shows a weight reduction for a very few amount. However, the number of evaluations must be increased. After that, this is turn of the other new five patients to be registered. The patient number 6 was a middle – aged teacher, while the number 7 was a kid, who tall down in the shaft enclosed their house. The patient number 8 was a young girl, who was dishonored in one street at city, has involved sever injures. The patient number 9 was a teen girl who went in comma due to drug overdose.

The patient number 10 was an old women, who apparently hospitalized due to her high aye and has experienced a sudden shock. Among those patient, I was looking at two teen girls, who could enjoy their teen hood instead lying on the bed. Seeing such a situation was making me sad, especially, the young girl who not only be dishonored, but also damaged either physically or psychologically. Even, police officers were saying they wanted to number her, but they could not due to arrival of police officers, I was depressed due seeing such conditions, as well death of the patient number three. I got beak home. As soon as my mother saw me, she got something mode me unhappy seeing the appearances of girl and sadness on my face, since, she knew I'm coming from the old house, she was thinking that something bad happened probably.

"My dear son, shall we walk for a while "she said.

I accepted her suggestion and we went to the garden together. Walking on that garden in presence of my mother was aspiring me a nice feeling. As I was passing the sidewalk, my toot hit it and my mother take my hand to prevent of my felling down "be careful my son "she said.

My father was watch on upstairs, he reached us and changed or walking to a family walking. "how could you walk to me, haven't you missed me? "My father said.

All of our three started to walk. I have not experienced such a good feeling for a long time.

In the middle of the way, my father was discussing my childhood memories for my mother.

He was emphasizing on the "you have not heard it "to interest her on what he was narrating. My father continued: when Sohrab was a child and has recently learned how to walk, I used to bring him to the park, I always tried to let him to walk some steps forward of me. That day, I was distracted for some steps and I saw Sohrab is not here! I was running from one side of park to another side to fide him, suddenly, heard the shut of closing the caput car and crying of the driver, and I turned to see what's going on. It seems the car has a technical defaced and the driver was trying to repair and test the motor, that the caput had been closed. Suddenly, I saw Sohrab he's strongly running and telling. "father run, I hit the caput on his head. "

My son and me as run as the man could not reach us. "really, did you run?" my mother said.

"actually, you know, I had to pay the cost of bringing his car to a mechanic workshop to forget It." my father said.

"Do you still remember this memory? "My mother told me.

A shout while, we got back home, I went to my room, changed my clothes, watching the outdoor behind the window and slept.

Tomorrow, I was the first person, who left the house. I went to the old house the results of yesterday night. As soon as I got there, I faced the caution signals, related to that kind elderly women, which me sad.

However, I should evaluate the experiment results accurately. There for, I tried to control myself.

I sat behind the monitor of her was evaluate ted too. I was sad seeing she is dying. However, the death is also something like birth and everybody must pass it in his way, suddenly, I remembered the face of that offensive man who died yesterday night, who was showing off the fear on his face. This women was a good human based on what I knew about her. I adjust her bed camera on her face and the desire, which can be seen was interesting for me, maybe, the birds have come to bring her, the birds who have eaten the suds of the kind women. Probably. I looked at her hands. They were open.

There was no wish to stay. Seeming she was appreciating the death, showing she is going to a place filled of peace from a place filled of loneliness. A few weight reduction also can be observed in this case. The weight reduction was observed in both of them. Is this weight reduction related to their spirits?

I looked at the other beds, evaluating the registered information in hospital forms, which obtained through connecting with hospital computer system. The 24 young man was a sport coach. He does not smoke, while some other similar factors confirm his heath before bringing him to this unit almost. Evaluating the death style of the patients' number 1 and 3 raised another question: is there any significant relationship between the drudge type and their good or bad characteristics?

To find out an answer for these questions, I should obtain some information from those who know them. What her they are good or bad people? Therefore I could get the addresses of each one a big problem. How about I go to their address and interrogation about them. From the other hand, it was better to research indirectly to stay unknown. However.

If I wanted to ask for help, the possibility of their cooperation of their cooperation was low, while its risk was high due to nature of my experiment.

I thought, the only way is changing my appearance to stay unknown, at the beginning.

It seems unpractical, because know anything neither about makeup, nor l have din it so far. Therefore, I started to study about make up. I bought several books, as well some make up tools from a relevant shop, and I was studying the books, while to do my first make up. It was not so good, but not too bad for the first time.

I got back home deciding to focus on learning of make up again. Today, I have tried to practice make up on the grim appliance, which made to hold wigs from the morning up to the noon. Therefore, I got a better control on make-up.

It was almost noon, the instruments started to send caution signals for the patient number tow. This patient was on comma, under such condition, evaluating dace of the patient could not be possible. Therefore, could only evaluate the patient weight. The weight of this patient also reduced a few. Three patients have died so far. However. The patient number 10, who was brought due to side effects of high age and the sudden shock was transferred to an ordinary unit. Some others were died or some were hospitalizing my studying on make-up. At night, I came back home. I get up soon in the morning, and come back to the old house with no time wasting. Within a short while the instruments connected to the patient. Number 7 meaning the child who fall down in the shaft beside their house started to send caution signals. I hope he got his health like that middle aged woman, and come back to his used life, however, not only he had so much of broken bones, but also the effect of breathing poisoned gases of the shaft also got severed. He died calmly. A few weight reduction also was observed in this case, I got back home at night.

While I brought the addresses of those five people on a piece of paper. Among them.

The image of dishonored girl continuously repeated on my mind. I seems she was asking from somebody to get her revenge.

Therefore, I decided to search about her and how she is dishonored first.

Chapter III

The teen girl

At night, I was thinking what kind of make-up I can choose, as well this fact my first experience of real make up how be. I got the old house in the morning. A simple make up including a hat and beard and mustache was selected. I tried to change more using clothes instead of a heavy make-up. The type of selected clothe was sport.

I went through the back yard of old house to not be seen, going to a bus station prudently. I reached where the girl was dishonored through metro and bus system. On that part of city, there was a park, and the bad event had occurred in a corner of Park as I guess. I sat in a chair, I had nothing except the address of event occurrence and her living place. I need more data. Online was a book store with online free book searching system? I was also made up and no one could recognize me.

I decided to get a part of my target data through another way. I went to that book center, I sat on a chair, browsing the site of local police station, continuing different stages. I studied her profile over there, I could obtain the phone number of a friend of her who accompanying her up to the ending moments. I noted it on a sheet. I went to her education place. Asking from his schoolmates helped me to find her.

However, instead of speaking with her at education place, I went to her living place directly, waiting to come back home. I was following her in their avenue. She was completely teared and it could be clearly understood. I reached her and stopped in front of her. "I have told nothing to nobody about what happened that day ". She cried. I was making sure her that there is no relationship between me and those people.

In addition, I told her what you tell me would remain a secret between us. At first, he was just denying, however, when I told, her worriedness is perceivable for me and I just want to punish them, she narrated the adventure of that night. "That day, as the school time finished, we were discussing the school project with each other. We went to a mall to buy what were needed for the project. We bought son of things we needed, so, we will reach our houses late. At we got off from the bus, we noticed a several boys, who haunt in the near park were following us. We should pass that park to reach our house. In the entry of the park we decided to run as we arrive the first turning, which was covered of tress to refuge from the boys. We could not run very well due to the tools, which we had bought. However, my friend was in front of me with a several step.

Since, I could not run very well from one side, and the space was dark due to sunset from the other side. I fall down.

I just saw, one of the boys could reach my friend throw her down severely, while the others reached kept hands and legs, while she was trying to save herself. I could do nothing. I hide in the bushes until they went. I came to our house, and I have told nothing to nobody due to fear of those sinter boys. "

She told these words and rapidly went toward her house. I come back to the old house, I removed my make-up and watched the monitors. No especial event. Has happened in the hospital. I should design a different morning, when I got up, I reviewed my plans. Then, I went to the old house, going to bus station and the hangout of the sinter boys.

I sat on a chair of park. Supervising everything. A several hours past. It was almost afternoon and nothing happened. I was felling hangout. I went toward a shop enclosed the park to buy chocolate, in the middle of my way, I saw a local seller, who sells small sandwich.

I preferred to buy a sandwich instead of burying chocolate to get back sooner and supervise on everything.

There were some steps between the sandwich kiosk and me, that one of those boys make up and got back our home, when I got up. It was morning, when I got up. Although I self-sleepy. I went to the old house to prepare myself for another day. As I entered the patient number 5 who was incurable was showing the caution signals. I told to myself a good is not waiting for me! Some moments later, that child died too.

The weight reduction happened as usual. I was almost ready to go to the park. I could obtain some information about the boys who dishonored the girl – like where they live through questioning and supervising.

However they living place was somewhere which was considered as the hangout of addicted and homeless people, while if somebody else went there, the inhabitancy bothered. also perceived two of them are brothers, as well the ether three were brother too, their boss was the older brother of the group including 3 brothers, who gives then drug to sell for him. He may use the obtained income to buy new drugs or to supply the costs of group. When I was coming back to our house, I was thinking that I cannot use the such a make-up, which changed me to the inhabitants of there.

Supervising then for several day showed me they usually stag.in their hangout up to the afternoon, if I wanted to check their house, I should do it before afternoon.

If was morning, and I had enough time before going to their living place. I looked at the list of people who were on that unit. I decided to aged women. It seems, she comes from side of a charity intitule to the students, she was brought to the hospital due the hits and resulted injuries of those injuries from side of some unknown people. I went to the old house, I single made up my self, although my make-up was simple. However, I took about too hours to finish. That was not perfect abut not too bad, and better the past. I went to the school, when she had worked. I was standing near the school and wondering how I can find a student, who were the middle-age consider too. There was also something wore for this case. Police was interrogating about her align to me. Therefore, if I did something about her along to me. Therefore, if I did something wrong without prior planning, I would be accused, while I would not get my desired data. I passed around the school, as well evaluating the interior space to arrive in the built in, which was installed on the wall, I understood, the intra – matches will be held tomorrow. I thought this is the best time to do my research far away from the demanding sights of there anymore due to curious sights of students. In addition, I should come back to the old house and prepare myself far today afternoon to go to the house of those felon boys. I changed my self to a homeless. However, passing through our avenue was a little hard due to the homeless appearance. I prudently brought an agreeable set of cloth and put it on the pack, I was bringing, and finally, I reached my target house. There were some old houses and abandoned up to these people illegally inhabited them.

Such a condition provided them this opportunity to get them. When the felon young men arrived in there. When the felon young men arrived in their housed. I saw, two of them were verbally arguing, which shows there are some sever problems and difference among them too.

There was a kiosk in that port avenue as a retail. So, I went there. This kiosk had the best overview on the avenue. I sat there pretending I'm sleeping to prevent to be paid affection me. The owner of kiosk was trying to prevent of my keeping over there at first. However, as he faced my emphasizing, he finally forget it and came back to his kiosk. I was not only supervising on their house, but also paying attention to the kiosk indirectly. It seems he got more money comparing what he sells. I perceived this fact as someone as somebody came to buy something, this issued caused to attract my attention rather than their house. I supervised him for a while, and I understood he informs the others of commuting of strangers, in this case they could sooner run or prepare themselves for a fighting if.

It was necessary that extra money, that he receives, in fact, was his wage. The presence of this man makes difficult to penetrate in their house or seems impossible.

It was pasted a long time of night. But the conditions were in such way that I could not go back home. Therefore, I stayed there. It was about midnight that an old car stopped in front of their house, In return for a plastic bag, he gave them a box. He came to the kiosk, and the first thing that asked the owner of the kiosk was about me. "Who is that sleeping here? " he said.

"A homeless, worse luck than you." The owner of the kiosk also said.

Then, they bought a soda and paid more money to the owner of the kiosk, like other people who came to the kiosk. "Have you gotten these weekly sales quotes? " The owner of the kiosk, while counting the money, said. "They are good sellers, I have brought them twice as many times as I did, this time." The man said

Saying this sentence, he drove his car and went off. It would have been understandable that he meant the narcotics for the materials, that the boys sell in the park every day. Some whiles later, the conditions for leaving that place were provided. I returned to the old house. I changed my clothes on the way in a corner. I walked through several streets going to a taxi station near the old house. Two of three streets remaining to the old house, I left the taxi. Because I thought I should take caution.

I got an old house and changing my clothes and cleaning my grin lasted a while. I looked at the monitors, it seems nothing bad has happened. When I returned home, it was almost morning, and I went to my room and I fell asleep as I tuned my bedtime. I should not lose tomorrow's school competition, the alarm clock could not wake me up due to the low hour I slept. Finally, my mother, who was passing by my room hearing the alarm woke me up. I still had enough time to reach the inter-class sports school, but I had to hurry. I went to the old house and made up myself. I went to a shoe shop and bought a pair of expensive shoes for my afternoon plan. I remembered how much I had tried to get the number of the foot shoe of the felon boy, which I chose for this part of my plan.

I had gone where they choose to stay in their hangout. Then I measured their foot trace using a ruler to get the number of shoes. I could get the shoe number according to the shoe model he was wearing. After purchasing that shoes, I reached the school with too much of sufferance. I went straight to the school sports ground. I should have chosen a place to sit among the students of that counsel. Once, I heard from the two hospital nurses talking that the counselor was teaching at the last high school level. So I had to sit among them. I highlighted the place where the students of the upper secondary school were sitting among them looking at the tournament. Since the parents and the students' families also came to the tournament, there was no problem with presence of me there. Everyone thought I was a member of the family of a student. When I talked with students about Ms. Counselor, I could not ask my questions completely because of unwanted attraction of the attention of other people. As far as I could, I asked them questions. I thought to investigate more about Mrs. Advisor, I could go to the parking where the accident occurred as the tournament is running. I was looking for her car and I hoped it was still there. I found the car. It was still at the scene of the incident, I watched it all around carefully, while I had to be careful not to attract others' attention. I could find nothing significant around the consultant's. Under the eyes of all students who were constantly moving in the parking, accessing to the car dashboards had a high risk. In addition, I was sure that its contents had to be checked by the police. There was only one other place that could be related to the Ms. Consultant, which was the consultant's wardrobe. I arrived into the school hall, many teachers had gone to the gym. Therefore, the school was quieter rather the usual. However, the school principal and moderator were in conversation looking at the schoolyard from the office window. In fact, that conversation could not be considered a conversation between the two, the moderator were confirming, whatever the school principal said!

I sat in the chair behind the office looking around to find a way to get to the consultant's wardrobe. Suddenly a police officer entered the school corridor and went to the office. I could hear their talking and perceived the contents of the wardrobe and the consultant's car were transferred to the police department for further investigation, so, there was no need to find a way to reach the consultant's wardrobe. However, I realized the director's request for a police officer to come to school from the conversation of Mrs. Director, was that the counselor's mobile phone had fallen into a fallen garden at the time of the conflict, and a student delivered to the school's moderator this morning. The police officer urged the director to charge his phone as they provide the required condition to transfer the car, so that some important information could be obtained. Then he left the office going to the parking lot. The manager and the moderator fortunately went to the sport field to check the matches. It was the best time for going to the office investigating the mobile phone of the consultant. I was surprised to see she had determined no code for her phone, while erased all the data, which no longer needed them. I did not have too much of time, I had to get out of the office sooner. As I review the mobile phone, the only data I got was an email address and a few phone numbers from the students. For me, these clues were enough. In the corridor, I saw the director and Mrs. Moderator were in conversation, while the manager was surprised to see the consultant's phone was in a garden that was so far from the parking. I would rather listen to the conversation between the manager and the moderator. Listening to a few people's conversations was not my desire, but I have no other choice. I realized the consultant was a kind and kind person from their conversation. Meanwhile, police officers were moving Mrs. Counselor's cars, a number of schoolchildren and school staff gathered there.

I was also standing among them listening to their words that I noticed the conversations of two school teachers who talking about Mrs. Counselor. They also greatly show respect for counselor, and they were surprised that the incident had happened to him. I think it would be enough to investigate this consultant. Because four people considered s as a Nobel person so far. I left the school, returned to the old house, preparing myself for the plan I had this evening. First, I went to the house of those several felon boys; I threw myself down near to their house pretending to sleep. The owner of the kiosk came to me to prevent me from staying there, seeing I'm asleep went back into his kiosk. However, he was looking at me time to time. The clothes I carried with myself as a homeless were in the two large cloth bags. When I threw myself on the ground, I threw the two large cloth bags on the ground in such way that those bags prevented to be seen by the owner of the kiosk. At one convenient opportunity, I arrived into the felon boys' house yard after opening the doorway. Fortunately, there was a dent in front of the door allowed me to open the door without being seen. I got into the house; I should look for a secret place they had spoken when they were in their hangout. It was in the upstairs, the third stair. They had digged the stair placed their valuable belongings inside it. I found the money packages and got some cash from one of them. There was also an album of girls' photos at that secret place, who had been dishonored during this period. On took it too. I went out of the house with great care. When I was in the yard, I saw the owner of the kiosk was moving fast towards the bags. Apparently, he had been suspicious for my presence beside them, going to check that I was there or not, I had to reach there before him. While he was trying to cross the street, he stood up in front of him talking with him for a while. I reached my bags at this opportunity pretending to sleep next to them. The owner of the kiosk came up angrily and woke me up with a few strokes of my pretending sleep telling I have to leave. I left there too quickly.

I went to the park where they were hanging out. It was time for me to run my other plan. I woe the expensive shoes I had bought waiting until the bad guy to be alone, who I need for filing this part of my plan. I crossed in front of him in such way that he could easily see my shoes. I guess it was right. As soon as I saw the shoes, he came to me and first hit me with a few strikes, then put my new shoes off, while he put them on, leaving his old shoes for me. He was picking up my pockets and already had some of the money I had taken from their house to carry out this map, as well the remainder of the price of the shoes in my pocket. But he did not notice them. I threw them out of my pocket to see them. He saw and picked them up and put them in his pockets being happy to get that money. I rapidly took his old shoes to the shoe store hiding them in the trash near the shoe store in such way that could not be seen easily; going to their avenue. The sounds of their verbal conflict came from the house. When he saw me, he came to me and told others that he had taken the money and the shoes from me. Apparently, the rest of them were suspicious of the expensive shoes and the amount of money he had in his pocket. Seeing the money difference in his pockets, they were sure of that he stole them. To be got acquainted of this seeing me, but I told them that he bought his shoes from a shoe store that I was walking around in. He attacked me angrily and kicked me with some tight punches. The remaining of them stopped him, and one of them said, "Are you sure about that? "

"He even hided his old shoes in the trash bin near the same store. " I said.

They quickly mounted me on their cars, saying this. While the boy who took the shoes from me telling bad words for me. We arrived at the store where there was a fairly large distance from their house, I showed them the trash bin. We went to the trash bin and one of them began to scoop the garbage, when he saw that boy's shoes, he showed them to their chairman.

Therefore, the boy who had taken the shoes from me tried to shoot me with the gun. However, the three brothers threw their weapons and shot each other supposing he intended to shoot them. The brother, who took the shoes from me, shot them to defend his brother too. In a few minutes, the remaining of them had fallen on the ground except for their chief who had been shot too. I would certainly have been shot if I had not been hiding behind trash bins. Their head was taken to their car while being injured and fled from that place. I though he probably comes back home. I thought they would eventually beat each other for such an event, but they were crushed and killed each other. Hence, the girls' revenge would be taken. Perhaps this was the punishment of all their sins. I was filming of all this with the help of a small camera. Their chairman remained still. I got an idea. I have to reach their home. When I got there, I saw that the head's car was parked carelessly at home. I went to the kiosk owner saying I am looking for one of my accessories and asked what happened? He told me their director had been injured and returned home asked me: "do you think what happened to him? "

"They must have been involved with each other, the next intersection I saw one who said that they killed each other in a clash, their headmaster must have died so far due to the severely injured. " He took a gun from inside the kiosk hearing these words and went into their homes. I was sure he will do this. All the drugs and money they hid could tempt anyone surely. The sound of bullet can be heard from the house. After a while, both of them came out of the house while were stumble. Their head fell to the ground at the house, and died. The kiosk owner came with a bag of money to the kiosk, and then he died too. No one else dared to come out of their houses, I thought the money was surely the right of others picking it up and getting out of there. As I was walking away, I looked at their houses and saw one of their neighbors went to the house and left with a box of materials.

I changed my clothes in one of the two less crowed alleys of the two or three streets above. I took the bag and the photo album throwing the remaining items into one of the trash cans. I carefully returned to the old house taking care accurately I had not been pursued. I put those appliances in a corner on the floor looking at the monitors, none of the previous patients had died. Two new people were added. Patient No. 11 was a man who was injured in an accident, and the patient No.12 was also a construction worker who had fallen from the building when he was working in the building. I looked at the counselor's face on the monitor, which, in the perspective of her colleagues, was a respectable and Nobel person. After removing my make up, I returned home, my mother said to me, "what do you do that makes you so tired of yourself? ”

“It's not too hard to do! ” I said.

“You do not know that I've just gone to death just today! ” I was murmuring by myself.

During the period I went to change clothes and wash my hands and face, my dad came home, I decided to sit with them for a while talking about various subjects. Suddenly, the news of television showed the adventures of tonight. That news has saddened my mother and father were sorry for the incidents. “Presence of such people who endangers others' safety is a source of discomfort. ” My mother said.

“Absolut and strong deal will certainly be beneficial to such individuals. ” My father said confirming what my mother said. I was thinking, sometimes people should be more alert to avoid such phenomena at all. Of course, sometimes some policemen such as the police at the venue of the hangover does not have a serious deal with such cases are guilty too. I confirmed their words too. I went to my room and lay straight on my bed to sleep, without eating as the dinner.

It was morning as I opened my eyes. I went to the bathroom to take a shower. I still felt bad about the trash bins that I hid between them. I was looking as the blows, I was hitted yesterday in my mirror, and they were highly bruised. I was dressed to go to the old house. My mother took me in front of me and said: "As long as you eat breakfast I will not allow to go there. " AS I heard these words, I started to eat breakfast with her, but the blows I had hitted did not allow me to sit comfortably on the chair. It might have caused my mother to doubt it, so I quickly ate my breakfast and told my mother: "I think my muscle is damaged a little. " Although I knew my mother did not feel good about this, I went to the old house. I took the album related to the photos of the girls whom were dishonored by the evil boys harassing and looking each by each. I looked at the faces of the innocent girls who had fallen victim of some sentuals! I was looking at the photos, I had to pull one of them out to see one of those pictures, which was not clear. I accidentally looked at the back of picture. The address of the place of residence, first name and last name, and other details of that girl were written on the back of that picture. Apparently, these evil boys forced them to give their profiles after they harassed the girls to prevent them from going to the police. Using these specifications, written behind all the photos, I could help those girls. At least, decreasing their emotional discomfort a little. Their number was twenty! I wore a pair of gloves, to prevent my fingerprints remained on none of those items, I prepared twenty pocket packs, placed a movie showing how each one was killed in their own hands those evil guys. I also divided the money, which was a considerable money among them equally. I put the picture of each of these girls in that envelope. The twenty envelopes just got to hand the girl. I wrote on each of those envelopes using the letters of the name of the girl I saw from behind them, writing: "They came to the conclusion of their own actions - the Savior ."

The reason I used the title of Savior was that I heard it in that cave for the first time from the tongue of those creatures, which was questioned to me still. So it seemed to be fit my application of this title here. Now I should deliver the envelopes to the hands of those girls. I first needed a grim to not be known. The grim I had done was better than the previous times, then I left the back door of the old house. The first girl I had to deliver her the pack was working in a dry launderette. I got in and asked her a few questions about the time required to dry washing of clothes. Then I asked her to help me to bring my clothes. At first, she did not accepted to do that, but she accepted due to my insistence and came with me outside the store. Along the way, I put the envelope inside her pocket and asked her to wait for me to bring the cars containing clothes. She did too. But I went looking at him from afar. A little while passed, she realized that the envelope, which was inside her pocket; as she opened it and read it, started crying happily sitting there. Seeing the joy of other people was pleases me.

I should go to a school to give my second envelope. The second girl was working at a school as a grocer, as she was walking into one of the corridors to do her job. I said: "I'm sorry, lady, this package fell from your pocket." When she received the pack and was reading it, I quickly walked away from her, called me a few times, but without noticing it, I tried to hide from her. When she became disappointed with finding me, she sat on the edge of the school garden hugging the envelope looked far away. It seemed delivering the third girl's envelope was the most difficult. She works in a store as the cashier, so I could not give her pocket directly, because the risk that I was getting stuck was high. So I told a boy that if he did, I would give him some money

I half-folded the bill and gave him half telling to him, return to get half the other after as you gave the pack to lady. I put the other half on the banknotes there, and I went hiding myself to make sure he would give the pack to her.

I stole her door for a while to see the fourth girl and she was not there. Finally, a courier brought her a pizza order for her. I knocked myself on that motorcade, when he fell on the ground, I took the pizza and raised the pitch, let the pocket into the pizza packet, while the motorcade was very happy and thankful to see the pizza had not thrown down. As I was going I saw the girl was delivering her pizza. Likewise, I delivered the envelopes of all of them, except the envelope of the girl who was in the hospital.

Chapter IV

Ms. Consultant

This morning, when I went to the old house, a warning sound was coming from one of the monitors. I went to the monitor room finding out the alert was due to the patient No. 6, the same middle-aged counselor who had been injured by some unknown hits. Apparently, she first came alive from coma, but she immediately experienced severe symptoms and the hospital's recovery team was rehabilitating her. Because i had researched about he of the past, and her colleagues considered her a respectable person, I was more sensitive than others to see her face as she was dying, so I set the camera on his face. When she died, a great fear was seen on her face, but why?

Why should a person who was respected by her colleagues like this be so fearful of the death? If she was a good person why she was attacked by anonymous? Maybe I could get information from those phone number and email addresses of her, and investigating them have provide an answer to some of the ambiguities that have arisen in this subject. Unfortunately, the review of that email did not answer the questions raised, perhaps it seemed all correspondence inside it had been cleared by the counselor or anonymous person! However, why all his correspondence should be erased? I recovered her contact list. I sometime looked at the monitors I noticed that the teenage girl being harassed was thoroughly crawled. She was not fully aware of his vigilance, but I was waiting to get her envelope in a better condition to make her happy in this way. I made up my own. Over the course of these days, I have been adding to my skill every day and I have been trying to be more precise every day from the previous day in respect of make-up. My grim took some time because it was not well at first. I had to clean it up and make up myself again. In the final stages of my make up, I realized that the teenage girl had moved from that part to another. I should find her in the hospital. I went to the hospital. Since, the personnel knew me during my work time, I asked of some people. I could find that teenage girl.

Her parents were in the room next to her bed. I could not reach her easily. I should be patient. So I walked around for a while, as I realized that they had taken another injured man to the ICU. He was a police officer shot in a clash between several robbers and a police force. I listened to the words of the police officers who brought him to the hospital. Apparently, several armed robbers attack to a gold dealer in one part of the city, when they are going to escape, police arrives, then, an armed conflict starts between them. At that moment, armed robbers are firing officers, but one of the hostages was kidnapping a child to target another stranger. While the police officer hurled and injured himself. At this moment, I remembered the park policeman who took money from the evil boys and this policeman he was endangering his life to save his pedestrians' life. The thirteenth patient was a policeman who was hospitalized. I looked at the teen girl's room. Her parents were gone. I tried to enter her room without knowing it. I cut off the life that could inform the nurses. She was very scared to see me, I quietly put my finger on my nose, and she realized that she should remain silent, still she was not diminished in her fears, and I put the envelope out of my pocket and put it in her hand. Seeing the envelope inside her hand, she was surprised. I murmured you should not be worry about those who brought this problem for you. They got the punishment, which they were deserved. Hearing this sentence, she gave me a heartfelt thank-you note. I can saw a combination of surprise, fear and joy in her face. I told her i re-connect the ring and leave the room and I hope i will not see her again in the hospital. I felt her heavy sight on my body until I left the room. In the corridor, I saw her parents entered the room after me, after a while, her father rushed out of the room and came looking for me. But he could no longer find me, I left the hospital and returned to the old house. Immediately after removing the grim, I focused on the email address, after a while, I recovered the addresses that he was contacting with them and began to review them.

I immediately went to that e-mail address after clearing my grim. After a while, I recovered the addresses contacting with them and began to review them. Almost all of them belonged to his students. In the first ten addresses that I reviewed, it was only daily correspondence; but on several subsequent addresses I encountered a correspondence that was not normal. I could see a particular cycle. Whereas a letter was sent to the student by a middle aged counselor stating she was worried about her future course in a maternal and compassionate way! In the next letter, she helped the student to solve the student's problems and was asked if she could go to counselor's home for help classes and write an address at the bottom of the letter, but the address, which was presented as the consultant's home address, was not her home address. In fact, in the forms of the police department and the hospital, another address were written. This was the first suspicious case with Mrs. Consulting. there were two modes nn the following emails: If the student responded positively to the teacher's proposal for the classroom going to that address to remove her academic problem, then the subsequent letters would be in a threatening format, forcing the student to come to an address at certain times; while It was not clear where to go. Under the second conditions, if the student responded negatively to the offer of tuition classes, the letters would be cut off at the same time. I was surprised! If students had gone to middle-age counselor for tuition classes, why they threatened to go to that address then. I entered the school site seeing students who were threatened by middle aged councilman have experienced a severe academic dropout. Now it's time to go to the place with the new make up to see if it's not the real address of the advisor's house, so where actually the address is? Reaching that place I faced a strange view! That address was to a vacant house, it was very distant from the consultant's address. It seems It did not getting into an empty house would make a problem for anyone, so I was waiting until night.

As the night came, I took care of that house to make sure it is empty. I arrived prudently, taking care nobody sees me. It was empty inside, there were not even the home appliances. Seeing this empty house again, I asked myself why students should come to this vacant house. Why none of the students who came to this place were injured or damaged? If there was something wrong with the students, why did not anyone complain? Why should the students come to this empty house several times per month? It seems the empty house hides something that only the consultant and those students knew about. Perhaps the reason for the incident that occurred to Ms. Consultant was also through the same house. I began to look at that house with the flashlight. There was no suspicious thing. I went to the room, perhaps I had to go to the roof, but the roof was visible to all the places, and it was impossible to happen something, while someone has not seen it. The only remaining place was the cellar. I went there. In contrast to the first floor, where no traces of the presence of a person or people were in it, it was easy to observe the effects of the passage of a person or people on the steps below. The dust on the stairs showed the passage of people from there. As I reached the stairs, I realized the entrance to the stairs was locked at, but why? I had no device that I could open the door, of course, without damaging the lock. So I returned to the old house to find a way or a way. Breaking the lock leads the people who came to this place to be aware of the arrival of someone else in the building, so I had to find a way to open that lock without damaging it. I remembered that in the neighborhood of the villainous villagers, a locksmith, who had been asked by the addressees of the kiosk. I knew the address that the kiosk had given, so I returned to the old house. I made up myself to go to that dangerous avenue. It was night, but if it was going to try this way, this time was the best. I went to that neighborhood in a different way. I was in the form of another homeless.

Upon reaching that place, I looked at the kiosk, it was open, but another person was working there. This was the best for me. As long as he wanted to know the whole place and its people, my job probably ended up there as well. I went to the kiosk and said, "Did you come instead of the kiosk owner who was killed?"

"Why?" Without saying my answer said.

"Nothing I know my way." I said.

"At least, come and give me your share." He said looking at me.

I returned to him and paid a few money continuing my way. Apparently, the money was enough for him, because if it was little, he would certainly have asked me more money. During the few days I was on the side of the kiosk I learned a lot from that cursed neighborhood. For example, I knew that every person who needs the locksmith should show him three coins! I went to the locksmith's house and knocked. He asked from behind: “Who?”

“The locksmith, I need the locksmith.” I said.

He looked at me through a door gap, I showed him three coins.

“What do you want?” He opened the door and said.

“Let's go inside I will tell you.” I said.

I entered the house, there was very little light there, and less than anything could be easily seen. The locksmith asked me again: “What do you have?” I said to him: “I want to teach me to open a lock.”

He attacked me and said, “Go out”

“Do not worry, nobody except you can do it in this city”

“But you have to pay for it.” He said.

“I've saved some money in the recent months.” I said.

Of course, it's all the money, looking at the money that was in my hand and saying: “All this is, just a ten Benjamins”

I got up to get out, suddenly he said; “sit down.”

He brought a big box and said; “Find out the lock you want to learn how unlock it.” There was a box filled with various locks and I found that lock, he also taught me how to unlock it. When he finished his training, I wanted to go, the locksmith said; “You know, I’m not busy now as past due to new locks. The money you gave me is too much, and I am alone. So if you want, stay more, I'll teach you a few more."

He taught me to open a few other locks and finally said, "If you get 10 Benjamins, I'll tell you how to open all these locks."

"Ok, but you have to wait a while so I can get the money." I said him.

I left the house of the locksmith. I walked for a while, but I was only focusing on, whether someone follows me or not, either the people of that place or locksmith. I sat a little in a corner in order to make sure of. Then, I went straight to the house where the middle aged counselor took the students there with the same appearance. I entered it going to the clear. I opened it, but I was surprised to see that the underground was empty as well as the top floor. Why should they use such a big locked for that underground? I have to find a reason for this. I looked carefully all of the underground, as I was trying more, I would get less. I stood in the middle of the underground and tried to regain my focus. I got a new fresh idea, looking around and the dusts. I should follow the foot traces. Certainly, this footprint has gone somewhere and this could help me. I went to the underground entrance and followed the footprints were continuing on the floor.

In a corner of the underground wall, where lift was placed to lift the appliances to the upper floor, more footprints were ended. But I did not see the place where the lift was located on the top floor. All of the floor, even its rooms, I had searched piece by piece. Since, all of these footprints in the ground ended in this lift, then the answers to these questions should be on the same lift. There was only one way to figure it out. I should try that lift. I opened it easily, so I could easily get there, I turned on the button, but instead of going up, I went downstairs. As it stopped I opened it cautiously seeing there is an underground corridor with an altitude of about 1.5 meters and a length of approximately 20 meters. At the end of it, there were a number of steps up, walking into the tunnel and climbing the stairs. I reached a wooden door. It would be possible to see the other side through the door hole. When I looked at the other side of the door, I saw the other side of the door was a house too. Therefore, regarding the direction of moving in the tunnel and the length of it, it was to be guessed, that house should be the second house after the house I entered. I opened the door and looked at into the house. Its furniture was arranged in a special order, and everything was clean and neat. I had to enter the house taking the risk to know the rest of the story. I entered the house and started to review it. Everything was normal except the tunnel which I came in. I decided to return, but I always concerning no one would use such secret ways for a normal home. Therefore, I decided to look a bit more for the possible clues. There was nothing could attract attention inside the rooms, the kitchen, and even the bathroom. I was standing in the living room and looking around. Suddenly, I saw a sleep lamp mounted on the wall. Why should a sleep lamp be installed in the living room? I tried to turn it on. However, it did not turn on with any key of there. Apparently it was broken. I went to the rest rooms of the house. In each of the bedrooms, the same sleep lamp was installed, while none of them worked.

There were also other types of lights that did not work in the kitchen and bathroom! Perhaps this was the clue I should have followed. I looked for a key for each, but there was no such key. The number of keys of the building were equal the lights, while all of them were ok. Why should there be a light without a switch key. The only result I could get was that these lights were installed when the construction of the house was over. Their installation height was too low for a sleep lamp. I was closely examined one of them, my guess was right. They were not really the lights of sleep, but they were cameras used to capture images. There was a memory card inside each of them. I returned to the previous house. There were two of these lights there. One of them placed in the entrance hall and another one in the ground, I took their memory cards. I closed the lock under the ground and quickly got away from that place. I spent all my efforts to do this quickly and I was careful not to be pursue by anyone. I returned to the old house. Immediately, I began to examine the contents of those cards, from the entrance corridor to the basement and the next bedroom, respectively. What I was saying seems unbelievable. That respectable woman chose baits among the students in each class and then dragged them down with deception, showing herself deceptively sympathetic to their curriculum and tuition classes. She brought them to this place. However, she has also been a mediator, and she did not work for herself. He transferred these students to the next house through the underground, and placed them at risk for abuse by individuals who could not have been explicitly following their own hustle and bustle. It became clear that the reason that students entered the side of the house and then moved to the side of the underground corridor was that any particular person inferring from the movies would not know them. When they left the house behind them secretly there was no proof of any relationship between them. In fact, they establish such a project to ensure that the neighbors have not been suspected the students and their commuting.

In this way, certain people went to the house and the students went to the empty house. Then they were passed through the underground corridor to this house. So that no traces of the ugliness that they were doing would remain. But, she had tried to film these people at the time of committing the crime for what kind of reasons? Maybe to save her own life and perhaps because of the profits and extortion of those people. All of those actions that she had done in right of the unpardonable student for her own financial gain, lead to be feared at his death. The amount of movie that each of the cards were captured was limited to only three identifiable ones. It was almost morning I returned home and tomorrow I went to the old house around noon. I delivered a copy of those memory cards to the police department giving the explanations wearing the new makeup to prevent loss of rights of the students waiting for the result. The next day, the poor student in the movies was killed in a severe accident. I saw the locksmith body and two of his men were killed in clashes between evil people close to that house in the events of the events. Later, I realized they were pursuing me in that night, thinking that I was going to open a lock where a lot of money was probably hiding there. They went to the house where send by a middle-aged middle age counselor to trap the students the next day, to steal money that they thought there were. They were killed by unknown people who had killed the counselor. They were abandoned on the street beyond that home, and then it was shown in the news of the events as a clash between the villains. The next day after the locksmith was killed in a strange action. Both houses were destroyed to build new homes. The three people who were present in the film, one of them died suffering from a heart attack. The two others were transferred to other cities and no longer had I seen any traces of them. One of the two police officers who I gave them a copy of movie was killed in a clash with several robbers, and the other was promoted several days later.

The house where the middle-aged counselor was living, I realized that was secretly under the control of unknown people as I was crossing over, and they all brought me a lot of experience. I was in the old house looking at the monitors were there. At this moment, Sayna interrupted me; "These incidents are not really easy to be believed."

"I know believing what you heard would be hard to you. However, you should know that I have seen all this on my eyes." I said to Sayna. I got up from place and told him; apparently this time lasted a lot comparing the previous times and I think it's enough for today. Sayna accepted. I took to her room and I went to my own department

Chapter V

Insulated beds with antimatter insulation

As usual, I went to her room and narrating what happened. I told the middle aged counselor was apparently respected by many of her colleagues, but when I involved into her life, I saw that she was a very bad personality, which is really unbelievable. Nothing special had happened as I was looking at the screens. Therefore, I could easily examine the results of changing weights. In all cases, weight variation was low, but as it was known that weight change occurs when a change in the material forming body occurs. As we know, W = mg. As it is clear from this formula, the value of G was the same before and after the death of the individual, so we should be changed based on the M change. However, on the face of the body, there was nothing to indicate that the dead body component was reduced. Since they were immediately weighted after death, we could not say that the reduction in body water or its corrosive processes affected patients by weight. So I should go to the hospital for further examination, but this time without a grim.

Upon arriving at the hospital, I saw one of the people who met him during the repairs of that part of the hospital. "Was the unit that our team had repaired furnished?" I asked.

"Yes, but some of the beds have been transferred to other sections, for example, the infectious unit". He said.

"What do you do to prevent infiltration of other parts?" I asked.

"We do the same with what you did to prevent dust from penetrating other areas! Nearly, one kind of isolation is created by using tents mounted on the beds, or the isolations we have for the whole of that part." He said.

Based on what he said I concluded that if I could use tents like those used for infectious isolation for hospital beds in that area, the removal of matter could also be prevented. I remembered several orders were ordered at the hospital's orders, which were ordered to equip the necessary unit in the hospitals. I got an idea. I could do like the previous one, so I had to go back to the old house. I was leaving the hospital, and I said to myself, "It's not so bad. I'll go to see the teenage girl who was harassed and see her. "

When I arrived in his room, she seems better, but still there was a bruise on her hands and her face, smiling at me, she said; "Sir, sorry, give me this glass?"

"Sure." I said. I went inside the room and gave her the glass. The glass was empty and I was surprised due to this request!

"Thank you, I saw the videos." She said.

I pretended I know nothing. "Which movies?" I asked.

"I do not say anything to anyone, The Savior." She said.

"How understood it?" I asked.

"When you do something good for someone, you've actually planted a grain in his heart, and this seed will grow up and surely; that seed will know her own the gardener." She said.

I said goodbye to her and got out of the hospital. I returned to the old house and started making designs for those beds with isolation. Nano scale materials should be tested for material that cannot cross the tent of these beds. For this purpose, I would first have to build a tent of beds for making. I looked at the monitors and I noticed the patient number 4, the middle-aged man I had not yet been careful about him. Looking at his case, I found that he was in a

coma for a stroke. The wounded police, who was number 13, had also been recovered from comma. He was still in the intensive care unit, and doctors told their colleagues that his recovery was low because his severity was too deep. I studied the properties of different materials. According to what was written there, only fluids could be easily moved, but provided that certain conditions were established, fluid flow through a solid object was also possible. However, its velocity was strongly influenced by parameters such as the degree of porosity and parametric in this solid material. Considering that, as the patient dies, weight loss was due to the outflow of material from his body, this material should inevitably take the fluid state, so the tile that was supposed to play the role of insulating antimatter should also be solid. The material also is ductile. It took me a few days before I was able to make a transparent material with the smallest porosity and formulation of a combination of several substances. To ensure that it does not pass through any material with a high coefficient, I sewed them using Nano scale materials from a company that worked in this area, and if the porosity of the Nano scale remain in them. After the preparation of these tents made of antimatter insulation material, it was time to design and construct them. The plan of this structure was a rectangle measuring 3 x 4 meters, which, on four sides, was tolerated by four columns of high structural loads.

On the one side, I installed oxygen capsules, along with filters for air purification that cleaned indoor contaminants leading into the surrounding area. In one part there was a compressor designed to store and store the domestic air after the refrigeration when needed. In this case, the oxygen capsules provided the patient with air. There were also sections in which all the needed and consumed items were placed inside the isolation space and their weight; while their weight were measured and determined. For waste garbage, special waste bins were installed inside the isolation space so that no material from the isolated environment was removed during the death of the patient, and the mass of the substance contained in that isolated space remained constant. There were spaces for access to the indoor environment that the physician and nurse could access the patient without having to enter the isolation space to examine or give them medication. In this way, unauthorized entry and exit were prevented from isolating the space. There was also a good number of bulbs in the appropriate tents to provide adequate lighting for the interior of the isolated environment when needed. I set up serum storage sites and set them up outside the isolation space, and the serum was directed through the special channels for each one to the interior of the isolated environment. I had done many of the necessary predictions to measure the weight of the patient, ensuring that the substance was not removed from the isolated environment. To measure mass, I designed and fitted a scales in the shape of an umbrella at the bottom of the isolated environment to measure the weight of all the objects that inserted the interior of the isolated environment. In all parts of the body, ceiling and floor, a set of barometers was installed. This was because if the body exits the soul, the body of the patient, if it has a material condition, will leave pressure in the body of the tent to enter the isolated environment in case of contact with the antimatter insulation and will force it, which will be measured by these pressure gauges.

Therefore, if the soul has a material state, it will be imprisoned in the isolated environment after leaving the body and this will leave the soul out of the body when it leaves the tent. Regarding the tent is isolated from the insulating material, this exhaust from the tent will be pushed into the tent by pressure and this pressure is measured through pressure gauges. It took us two days to embed sensors of temperature and motion sensors etc. In this isolated environment. As previous beds, the camera and the microphone were embedded inside and outside of the environment, there were also sections that transmitted the vital signs and measured data to the lab. For the inside, I built the beds that I had already built, and after completing the entire design, I designed all the parts as folding and detachable to be suitable for field hospitals. I looked at the hospital order to manufacturing Bed Company. The delivery time of the isolated environments was ten days, so I worked twenty hours per day to build all the beds so I could prepare ten beds of them equal to the order of the hospital. On the ninth day the beds were ready. I went back to the orders department of the hospital manufacturer company. I changed the destination for the beds for the hospital to the old one, and I also issued another bill for my beds to the hospital. After being delivered in the section I got the orders from the hospital bed manufacturer on my website and I returned the addresses back to the first place. Finally, I went to the warehouse with a grim and a change of looking. I changed the address from the old house to the hospital manufacturer. In This way everything was set in motion, and the beds of my own making were replaced by those hospital beds.

Chapter VI
Police Officer

After I handed the isolated beds to the hospital, I had no hope of being used soon.

I looked at the monitors as well the results that during this period I could not carefully review them. Of course, all these results were recorded in the central computer and processed digitally. The experiment I was doing was divided into two parts: The first part examines the weight change of patients when they die. The second part examines the relationship between the lives of individuals associated with the difficulty and ease of the death of the patient. In the first section, I got almost the desired results, and in addition to processing the data by the computer, I reviewed the data recorded every day. But the second part was more difficult. Because it required field research. This time, I was looking for an investigation into a policeman wounded in the clash with several armed robbers. By studying the case, I found that the police officer's place was in the same neighborhood I was living. I came back in the shape of a homeless with a different looking. I went to the kiosk. I sat down next to the kiosk looking around. "I'll follow a key maker." I said.

"I do not know such a person." He said looking at me. I remembered that one person had introduced me to get an address from the kiosk. So, I told him one of the names I had heard before, hearing his name; "He's gone from this place, how had he told you to come here?"

"Because he's gone from here, he's told me come before you, otherwise he would take me to him." I answered.

He was almost convinced and gave me the address. Before I went there, I gave her ten sticks as it was common over there as kiosk right.

I went to the house of the second locksmith, who was most specialized in opening new locks and cash cow. I rang his bell door.

"What do you want?" someone said.

"I'm here to see the locksmith." I said.

He looked out of the doorway and I showed him three coins.

When I opened and went inside, he saw me saying, "Have you heard what happened to the head of the locksmith of this neighborhood?"

"No!" I said.

"After he instructed how to open a lock to somebody, he and his students followed him in order they might reach out to him from the place where the client wanted to open the lock, instead they were killed in that house." He said.

"Poor man, he got nothing for his life". I said.

"Regarding the fate of the previous Locksmith, I'm not telling you why you want to learn key words, and not who you are, and you do not know me after learning." The new Locksmith said. I accepted his conditions. I gave him the money wanted and began to learn how to unlock various locks. I asked him about an hour later; "Do you know the police who worked at this place?"

"Why are you asking this question?" He looked from the top of the glasses and asked.

"When he was shot, I was there, stopped in front of the bullet, and so that the bullet did not go pedestrians, I do not think that it was a bad guy." I said.

"He was a good man, he has worked for some time in the neighborhood until he was involved with a police officer who was taking money in the nearby park of thieves and bulldozers. He wanted to stand in front of him. " The locksmith stopped of the explanation of the lock and said.

"How did he want to stand against them?" I asked.

Apparently, the corrupt police had been reported to a higher position, and since they were also involved with corrupt policemen, instead of punishing him, they wanted to stop the good police colluding among themselves." The locksmith said.

"He was a good policeman, even sometimes, he would return the money that the corrupted police had taken from the people by force." He said:

"What did he do at the next street where the street is insecure?" I asked.

"He tried to stand in front of the criminals on that street, but all the criminals of that street, considering that they knew that he was a good person and even involved with corrupt police. As well the criminals were not happy with the corrupt police, they decided not to commit other offense in the street where he was working. They were also kind to him." He answered.

"Those robbers were not from this neighborhood. No one shots him at this place. " He said.

"Now the guys of this place are looking for the robbers and they will give them a good lesson soon, first because they shot him and secondly they were kidnapped in a neighborhood other than their place." After a long silence he said.

"If I find those robbers, I'm the first person give him his punishment." Then the locksmith picked up and punched the wall and said.

"Indeed, he paid a monthly amount of money to the store to provide several homelesses and several street children from there." He said looking at me.

"Why did not he give them money?" I asked.

"To preven them from spending that kind of money for drugs and cigarettes. You know, he was the model of some of these street children, and they wanted to be good police as he grew up." He answered.

"It's better to continue our work." Told me.

After leaving of that place, I was only concerning, I have not been chased like last time. When I arrived home, I was in the same vein as my mother called me and said; "Get ready to go to a friend's party together tomorrow night."

"Ok, I went to my room." I said.

The next night, along with my mother, we went to a friend's party. My mother introduced me to her friends and introduced them to me. I asked about one of my mother's friends that I had never met her and my mother said: "She is my old friend, along with his husband, who is the police chief of the city."

When I saw him, I got an idea, it might be better to speak with him about the good of the wounded police officer instead of sitting there. I started the conversation with him at one convenient time. I asked him the general condition and asked him about the city, as she said: “Police officers are doing their tasks in the city.”

Saying this, I confirmed his words and said: “Yes, I've heard a lot about your officers, and I fully explained to him the story of the police officer who was wounded in the hospital. I also said the story of the children in whom the dangerous neighborhood have chosen him as their own models and wants to be like him in the future. ” The story also brought several officers in the park to receive money from criminals. After telling the events for him, he asked me: “How are you aware of these events?”

"The story of several officers in the park can be asked from the kiosk at the park, and you can ask the warder about the wounded police officer or street children and homelesses.” I said.

“You were at that workplace?” asked me again.

“These events have been described from tongue of a homelessness, which has seen them all in his own eyes.” I said.

“If you wait, you can hear the result of these adventures.” He said.

And after saying this, he quickly left the party. His wife looked at me surprised, my mother asked me: "What did you say to him?”

“We talked about a few different topics, and he will be back for a while.” I said.

When the police chief returned and came to my place. He thanked me and said; “Those corrupt police were introduced to the military court. I do not think it would be possible to give him the medal of the police officer because they have informed me that he has died, and he must get a good answer in the other world."

After the party, we returned home. I woke up in the morning and went to the old house. I wanted to see the face of the police officer when he was dying, so I looked at the film taken from his face. The moment of martyrdom, he was very quiet. Perhaps his actions in this world were welcomed in the other world. I dressed the clothes and went to his funeral. At his funeral, a number of street children were standing in a corner and were respected by military rule. In addition to them, several houses were tearing in a corner and the owner of the neighborhood store also came. Some people in the area who were offenders were watching the ceremony in a farther car. After the ceremony I went to the old house. Apparently, at that time, the patient number 12, who is, the construction worker, had recovered and moved to another unit.

After the ceremony I went to the old house. It was written in her case that he would probably not have the ability to move until the end of his life, but I hoped this would not happen. There was also a slight weight decrease in case No. 13, the police officer. I planned to go to the residence place of one of the patient to check the past and the life. He was the patient number 4, a middle-aged man who had had a stroke. His place of residence was in the center of the city. I went to his bookstore after changing my look. His bookstore was small, I went to the bookstore and picked some books. I went to the sales student to pay for books. The bookstore was quiet and I asked the bookseller's apprentice about the bookstore owner, the bookstore student seemed to be a little distressed, so he began to talk. The bookseller's student said the bookstore owner is a kind person who has loved him too much. But five years ago, when his wife betrayed him, he remained unmarried and kept himself in a bookstore. Until the end of this tragedy brought such a problem to him. At that time, the student showed me a year ago picture of him, and immediately showed me another picture of the sales book a few weeks ago. Comparing these two pictures, I realized it was like 20 years these 5 years. When I saw these two photos, I was very impressed, and on the way I thought of how the treachery of fire had managed to destroy the life of that loyal man. I reached the old house. I concluded that humans mask their faces to show themselves as they wish, but you will find only one thing behind each mask, which is their truth. While I went to study the life of the book seller, three new patients were transferred to this department. Patients Nos. 14 and 15, who had two young boys who were not well versed in the use of pill packs and were transferred to this section. Patient No. 16 was a young woman who had been transferred to the car by accident. Approximately an hour later, and at a very short distance, the two young people died. The reason for their deaths was the high consumption of psychosocial drugs and late arrival to the hospital. Both of them showed weight loss, but due to death in anesthetic state their faces were unclear.

Patient number 11, the man who was also hospitalized in a car accident, died this night. At the time of his death, there was some slight weight loss. This morning, when I got to the monitor room to see the monitors, the patient number 16, the young woman who had been transferred to the section after the accident, had now recovered and moved to another part. But the man of the book sales became more aware of the past days. His eyes were open, but he did not take long enough to see the warning signs on his monitor, and he was gone, his eyes were scared, actually too much. But why? As his student said he was a fan of affection, and he was very kind to others, he has saddened the past five years with the treason his wife has given him. He has not also left the bookstore and his home. Yes, that was the answer. His grief was due to cruelty to himself. He was as cruel as to himself that he was dying with fear. I decided to ignore the relationship between the life of a person and how to die. Maybe I would check this out at another time. This was the last patient who was hospitalized at that time, so I also had the time to release the next patient for other things. It was still a while since the unit had been left empty for a short time, 3 patients had undergone surgery and 2 patients had been injured in a street strife were brought. Fortunately, 3 patients who had been transferred to this department after surgery were recovered and transferred to other units. Of the two who were injured in a street strife, one was transferred to other unit after a relative recovery, but another died. It also showed a slight decrease in weight. In the next few days, things were going the same way every day, but for me, something of particular importance was the isolated spaces. I started to explore the isolated spaces again and reviewed their details. I looked at their doors this time. In the entrance, I actually designed them so that if the spirit left the body of a human being has a material state, in the first step, the body barometers can record the pressure changes caused by their attempt to leave the tent with antimatter insulation. If they cannot register something. In the second stage, thermal and motor sensors recorded it inside the tent. But if they could not record anything, they would go to the tent door in the third stage. The door of tents were two parts: First the external door, which was located between the corridor space and the open air, made of antimatter insulation material. The second part was the corridor covered with anti-insulating material on all sides of the ceiling, so that it was impossible to move the soul between them without collision! Especially in the middle of the corridor, all of these disciplines were placed in the form of a curtain of various disciplines. Therefore, if a materialistic soul wanted to cross them, it would certainly have been hitted by one of them and an unusual movement was observed in them. The third part included one door of insulating material placed between the interior space tent and corridor. So it was impossible to leave the soul out of this path without seeing it. If none of these sensors recorded anything, and also the input and output set did not show abnormal movement, the spirit was not materialistic. I was narrating the details of this tent and beds that Sayna said; "Let's talk about this later, let's talk a bit more about insulating material?"

"This property is anti-material and in all materials in the world." I told her.

To better understand this property, we can use one example: As we all know, there is a heat transfer property in all materials in the world, and we use a coefficient called heat transfer coefficient to express the heat transfer property. If the amount of heat transfer in a material is of a higher value, we call it a good thermal conductor and if it is less than a certain amount, then it is called thermal insulation, and between these two quantities there is a wide range of materials. It's also important to know that even thermal insulation materials pass through some heat. The conditions here goes same, the material passes through each other, and each material has its own permeability coefficient. If this coefficient is greater than a certain value, the two materials are good conductive materials relative to each other. Example: If you drop a drop of oil from the bottom of a water container, it will easily reach the surface of the water, and if the permeability coefficient of the two materials is less than a certain amount to one another, they are read as impervious. Of course, no matter how much less permeability to each other, they are not insulated with each other! Only the duration of infiltration increases. In antimatter curtains, since the duration of the review is low, the material is assumed to be insulator than the hypothetical material that is the same spirit. Because the passage time is long. The main difference between the heat transfer coefficient and the permeability coefficient is the heat transfer coefficient, which is the number of a given number. However, the numerical permeability coefficient is a computational calculation which, given different parameters such as the density and heat transfer coefficient and etc… for each material separately. It is calculated and not specific for any material, but relative to each other in relation to each other. Hence, it will not be difficult to build, but later you will know it is very necessary for many new sciences.

Chapter VII

The Ring

This morning, when I went to her room. I noticed that Sayna was skeptical about asking questions. "Do you have a question?" I asked.

"A few days ago you showed me a design of the corners of the column in the house, which you designed. Can you show me the other parts of the pillar? " Sayna asked.

"Of course, but which part is more attractive to you?" I told her.

"When I entered the room for the first time, I saw that to activate it, I had to pour liquid light from one cup to another, so I would like to know how the same section is in the house you designed? " Sayna answered. We first went to the archive of pieces and brought out a box from the closet. The box was small, Sayna asked, "Is this box small to do this?" Sayna asked.

"The size is not matter, what is important is the process which is done." I answered.

We sat on one of the chairs in that section and opened the box. I took a ring out of it and showed to Sayna. I could see a surprise in Sayna's eyes. This ring was actually composed of two rings collapsing on each other, which consisted of two perfectly symmetrical rings placed in each other. They were made of a special solid crystal, which was more solid than diamonds, while instead of a jeweled, the two sharp sections that had left the body of the ring to each other were placed. I was sure that the questions of Sayna will be started. So I started the description for Sayna before asking a question. I told her I consider different stages to design this ring: in the first stage, the material of its constituent material should be chosen from the material in which the properties I wanted were presented. Therefore, I used a pure light conductor material that is several times harder than diamonds. After choosing the material's composition, I have to think to activate it. You see these pointed appendages that are placed on the ring instead of jewelry. Each of them begins to produce light when the boy and girl get the ring for the first time. The energy required for this also taken from the individual's body and his feelings directly. Exactly, same as what you've seen in your chandeliers, with this difference that it's very responsive to human emotions. The more love of couple to each other, resulted in the greater glitter of this magic jewel. The feelings of the two will show their emotions to each other. So that if they missed each other it will change in blue and if they are worried about each other, it will be changed unto yellow. It will also change in its own colors for every emotion. In this way, two people who love each other without obligation to explain something, their rings will express their emotions. In the next step, each one of the couple should put his hand on an orb in the entrance of the door. In such way that the ring is placed on a special place where is intended. At the same time, the central and smart home system detects the symptoms and begins to record the characteristics of the couple.

Thus, the heart that is embedded in the central part of the house turns on. According to this sign, all light conductor materials that are place throughout the building will be activated and take their light from the control center of that building, which is the bright heart. One of these units is the heart arteries we've seen before. After this, the relationship between these circles and the control center is established and remains until the loops maintain contact with the control center of the building, while the building's heart remains bright. But if one of them is separated or no longer be connected, the connection between the loops and the building is cut off. Therefore, the heart of the building is turned off, the other parts will gradually turn off and the building will die.

"But where do the rings bring energy to shine?" Sayna asked.

"From the body, which has it." I answered. Then, I cut the conversation.

After explaining this story, I took Sayna to another room.

"Where are we going?" Sayna asked as walking.

"Toward a room, which pleases you surely." I answered.

When we reached the room, a face appeared on the door and said; "Welcome... Please come in! "

As soon as she saw the room, she happily jumped up and down. "Every doll that I've ever had since childhood are in this room." Sayna told.

"And all the stuff I've ever had since childhood!" I said.

My goal of collecting all my childhood toys and Sayna's dolls in that room was that I knew that every human inside has an inner child, while as much as the age of a person goes up, this inner child will still remain in the human.

Perhaps it is necessary for the person to be perfect. We all have seen fathers playing with their children. In00 fact, these fathers through help of their inner child. As much as the child has better grown up, the father makes a more beautiful connection with his child in these situations. You have not seen any father who plays with his child through his grown up own. On the other hand, I tried to collect toys in this room that we have played with them in the past. Because there are memories behind each of these gadgets and it would be very enjoyable for people to remember the good memories of the past. We stayed the rest of the day in that room, and both of us knew that most people in their lives did not know any time for their childhood sweets. So the best way to forget the hardships of the current life is to return to childhood memories. It can be enjoyed with infinite enjoyment with toys under the best conditions.

Chapter VIII

The train

Today, I began to define what happened to me without any introduction. Perhaps the permeability coefficient is impossible from the viewpoint of many people, but something should not be forgotten that the penetration of the two materials into each other can be very small, i.e., at the surface of the particles of electrons and atoms. Perhaps, on a smaller particle scale, the material permeability coefficient is considered to be part of a scientific branch. At least, the penetrability between the two materials is equal to zero, and in most cases the permeability between the two materials is equal to one as maximum. However, the zero value does not indicate the lack of permeability, and only reflects the long duration of this penetration. This coefficient has many uses. For example, high-cost alloys can be made using this science at a very cheap price, and even there will be a catalyst for the penetration of these materials, and through this science, new materials called Meta materials appear in the field of science and knowledge.

Meta materials are a variety of materials that appear and expand on the basis of the penetration coefficient of the materials.

"This discussion is somewhat complicated. Is it possible to explain it to me using an example? "Sayna suddenly said.

To better understand these materials, I can explain that people in the world are always trying to use every science and technology for their own benefit. One of the most dangerous parts is Meta material. If Meta materials are used in the military industry, it will create new types of weapons as they are new. For example, if Meta materials used to make a bullet. The coefficient of permeability for building materials is one in the bullet, but the penetration coefficient is zero compared to human body tone. When a gun person fires into a house where people are hiding there, all the balls pass through the walls of the building. This happens due to their permeability coefficient relative to each other. While in dealing with humans, the Bullets create a gap and hole in the body of those individuals in order to open their path due to the zero permeability coefficient. Therefore, if these materials are used in guns, the other people will have no shelter to hide against these bullets. In addition, in this type of war, only humans have been killed and houses and towns remain healthy and intact. So these weapons will kill the most people with the least damage to the cities. Think of an explosion of a rocket made of Meta materials in a city. In this case, only humans in that city will be killed and will not be harmed to the city. After cleaning up the traces of blood and the remains of the human beings, the next people will live in it! "Never give anyone the secrets of making this material even me." Sayna looked at me at said.

"If you want Ok." I answered.

It was a few days in the hospital that the days were passing routinely normal. When the patients are transferred to this unit; some of the patients recovered to continue their treatment to other units, and some died after some days of hospitalization. But the results obtained were almost the same. Despite the passage of days, there was still no use of any of the beds with an antiseptic insulation tent, and I was waiting to see the result of their use. Some days passed in this procedure. As if the situation was not supposed to change! Until I heard the news of a passenger train carrying a chemical train and leaving its rails on TV news, I quickly went to the old house and looked at the monitors. The emergency state was announced. I was sure the use of isolated beds was rarely happen. Therefore, there should be no mistakes in the recording of the data submitted, but in this situation almost every ten beds were used. Isolated beds quickly were sending the measured data to the lab. Due to special conditions of the isolated beds, the patients were severely injured were hospitalized in them and treated. many activities were carried out in such a way that people in the tents rarely came out of it due to the smoke from the fire of the train carrying the chemicals. The activities were carried out outside the tent, and the air inside the tent was also provided by factors that were predicted for this purpose. The first injured died, ten minutes after the wounded was hospitalized. Motor and thermal sensors and with regard to the anti-foam insulation used, no material was found outside of the tent. Regarding the parameters measured inside the tent, no material, including solid, liquid or gas, was imported or exited. In this bed, all the evidence showed that the human soul is not material, but still, the weight loss of a person was seen before and after death. If the human spirit does not contain matter, then what is the reason for the observed weight loss? This was the first injured. I wanted from deep of my heart, the rest of the wounded be recovered. But I also needed more data to test myself. I had to wait, the number of wounded in this incident was high; on the other hand, the bed of No. 2 was injured, but it was not good at that time.

The number of rescuers and doctors in the area was low. Since the wounded were severely injured in these isolated beds, they were given temporary treatment and treatment. The injured, who were better offered taken to the hospital after undergoing outpatient treatment. Due to the large number of wounded, as the wounded man died, the first bed was transferred to another place and another wounded was placed in his place. Since the patient was hospitalized, a while needed to reload the bed was. During this period, the bed automatically measured the type and amount of the drug injected or given to the patient, his weight and the amount of mass that entered the isolated space and etc... were measured. The first bed was loading when the second one sent warning signs. Apparently, the injured second died, before the medical team could afford it, he died and valuable data was gained. We again had a slight change in weight, in addition, there was no data showing that the human soul had a material aspect. In order to be sure of the lack of souls in the material state in isolated spaces, I left a large number of strands made of insulating material into isolated isolates, but they rejected the presence of anything that has the properties of matter. These results and previous results showed that the human soul has no material state. So this question has always been raised: If there was no connection between the human soul and the matter, why was this slight weight change, anyway? The sound of warning signs from the 4th and 5th beds was also heard. I went to the monitor on the seat wheels and looked at the results and outputs of the two beds. Meanwhile, I received a three-letter alert from beds in the hospital's intensive care unit. These were the first injuries that had been transmitted to the hospital. It was a bad situation. The alert sound also came from another insulated bed, and I was going to them, when the other insulated bed sent the warning signs. When I got there, I saw that the isolated beds were Nos.7 and 9. Under that circumstances, the warnings of one of the beds were not finished yet, that another bed began to send warning signs.

I had a simultaneous alert for seven beds in the Unit. The condition I had never encountered from the first day of the experiment and brought two medical teams to the ward trying to save the injured. In the fifth minute after the first warning, one injured and died in the sixth minute five injured simultaneously. Of all, only one man's general condition returned to normal. I looked at other monitors. The 10th isolation bed was sending warning signs. A medical team went to rescue him, but apparently they could not do anything and he died. Nurses and hospital staff were relieving and transferring patients and were medical teams; they were doing their best. The injured people of isolates beds 4, 5 and 9 also died and should be replaced by new injured. Approximately, five minutes after the death of the wounded, and after confirming his death, the nurse came to the bed to separate the appliances and devices to prepare the bed to accommodate the injured. Despite all the devices attached to him confirming his death, he suddenly returned to his vital signs. Ignoring the bed number, I only found out from the camera pictures the bed was in the hospital's intensive care unit, but the nurse, while did not notice the signs of returning his symptoms, along with a number of his staff, take him to the hospital's refrigerator. I had to do something, otherwise he would surely die. I had to reach myself to the hospital quickly. My delay might have been led to his death. Without changing my look and feel, I brought it to the hospital. The hospital was under immediate conditions and there were a lot of wounded in different parts of the hospital. I went to the intensive care unit and asked one of the personnel where the died wounded are transferred. “They will be transferred by the doctor to the hospital's refrigerator after being confirmed.” He said.

In this critical situation, the situation is somewhat different, and accepting the dead person in the cold store needs more time. “How can I go to the refrigerator?” I said. He showed me the path. At the entrance to the cold store, a person who was also a cold-blooded person, tried to prevent me from entering, but as I explained him a little of the case, he also helped me find the injured. I found the wounded with him and went to the ICU, the medical team started to do the resuscitation process. I looked around. Apparently, the number of train wounded was so high, so I decided to stay in the hospital instead of returning to my laboratory, considering the Relief that I had passed, to help the injured. Many were volunteering to help the incident at that time. Helping the wounded was nearly completed, and the rest was done by hospital personnel. I went to the wounded man who I had saved him from the cold store, taking his profile and address of his place of residence and returned home. I was very tired so I slept very soon. It was nine o'clock in the morning that I woke up. After breakfast, I went to the old house to check the results of the experiments. I really wanted to have them analyzed and analyzed earlier. I was in the monitor room and I was printing and reviewing the results of last night's events. All of the reported weight loss cases showed a small amount. All pressure gauges and heat and motor sensors did not show any abnormal activity. Of the 20 injured people who were hospitalized on the beds that day, 12 people died and 8 recovered. And were transferred to the hospital for continued treatment. The number of injured people on the non-isolated beds was 50, of which 30 were transferred to other areas after their condition improved and 20 were died. I reviewed their individual data along with the videos I took from them. I think the data was sufficient to express the results, but reviewing all the videos and examining all the results for the patients and injuries took 5 days. I went to see the injured man who saved him from the cold. At the hospital, when I asked him to say that he was discharged from there, I went to his house. It seems he lives in that house alone, now one of her friends had come home to take care of him decided to take care him to recover his health completely. When I was talking the injured man saved of cold store, his friend asked me to take care of his injured friend for a while, as he goes shopping and returns, I accepted.

We started a conversation. I explained for him what happened inside the hospital and that she had accidentally gone to the cold store and then I saved him. When he heard these happenings, I could see joy in his face, and he thanked me for many times. "To tell you the truth, my goal to come was to visit you firstly, secondly, to ask you if you remember something from the moments you were dead or the moments you reborn?" I told him. "He does not want to remind that stream again." He said. Due to much insistence of me, he eventually accepted and began to explain. "He saw all the moments he was being carried by the relief group obscurely hearing the unknown sounds. When the medical team came to revive, he saw them, but he did not have the will to move and react at the hospital. I also did not have the power to stay in place until I have been able to move hearing the beep sounding continuously. But suddenly he realizes that he is moving upward rather than moving horizontally. It seems that the stretch and attraction that has already led him to the ground is not existed more and abandoned. However, some of that stretch remained in his presence still, which was considered an obstacle in front of his moving upward. When he looks at the force that draws him to the ground he understands sis body is on the bed." He said. So these events were sleep, or what he understood was moments after his own death, and what happened at that time was somehow a death experience. In fact, this is his own experience of his own soul watching his body, and sometimes this image is blurred from his body and sometimes seen as clear.

"How did you feel at that time?" I asked him. "Feeling so bad. Feeling a hitch that pulls me down and drives me back. Do I slept or awaken? Whether am I dead or still alive, such a feeling?" He said.

"How did you resurrected?" I asked him.

"The same stiffening or tensile strength suddenly increased and prevented my further climbing. Then it drove me down rapidly. In such way that I became unconscious of its severity. When I recovered I was in my own body again. I could see that hospital room vaguely .The next picture I saw was related as I was moving to the cold store. These moments are the hardest part of what I remember. Although I was sure of my being alive, but I did not have the ability to move. People who sometimes were commuting there did not pay attention to me. The idea that if I could not move myself and if I am moved to one part of that cold store, I would surely die of the cold. Definitely I would die. That part of the hall I was almost filled. That's why the less people were commuting there. I was slowly seeing the environment vaguely that I heard your voice coming to help me, you moved me to the related unit to revive me." He answered me.

"How could you find out that I am alive?"

"Accidentally." I said.

Now, his friend returned of shopping, placing his purchases on the kitchen table, he came to the room where we were talking. Since, I got the answer of my questions, standing on and said goodbye. I knew if he asks me again about how to know if he was alive, I might not find the right answer. "Please do not tell anyone what I told you." As I was leaving him he took my hand said. I assured him that these words would remain between us. After leaving the house, I went to the old house. I was reviewing the injured in the way. As he described, I conclude he had not died, only his soul experienced the departure of his body for some time. Why should he sometimes see occasions opaque and sometimes transparent? I went to the hospital to see the place he was hospitalized. I met a fascinating scene the intensive care unit. The bed used in the intensive care unit, which actually installed in order to predict the specific times was the same bed I received from the injured person who had been saved from the cold store. So the bed which I got the data was an isolated bed and not an ordinary bed. I went to the old house from the hospital going to the store to buy a few items. I was looking out of the glass shop until I got my turn to pay the price. Someone was cleaning the glass at the store, so half of the glass was clean and the other half was not clean yet. Therefore, it was possible that same sense of vision for clarity and clarity had happened for the person. Meaning, he was looking at his body through a clear object, so if his soul was suspended in the air, he could sometimes have been isolated inside the room and sometimes was isolated in the space outside the space. When he was isolated inside the room, he saw its body clear and clear, while he was isolated outside the space he saw his body opaque and obscure. So he has crossed the anti-insulating material several times. However, the antimatter insulation conditions or sensors neither changed nor recorded anything. All of them indicate the soul is separated from matter, at the same time, there is a close connection between the soul and the human body. I remembered the words of the Mother Emperor, who had spoken about the body and the soul. So I decided to go to ask a few questions. I went to the airport and with the first flight I was able to take I got the previous city of our place. I got a taxi to the address outside the city and moved there. The address I gave was such that the driver should cross the path near the cemetery, I also several taxis to get the same place align the cave passage. Finally, I got there. We get the cemetery after a while. I asked the taxi driver to stop the taxi near the street. I could clearly see fear in the taxi driver's face! He was right. It was night asking him to stop near an old cemetery in a road outside the city. "Have not we reached the destination yet?" He asked me.

"I'll get off right there." I said.

"It's been a graveyard." He replied me.

It was as if he wanted to tell me this truth if I did not know where I was going warning me in somehow. I thanked him and entered the forest. I continued moving on the cave until I reached the cave. I stood in front of the cave entry, the crater was closed, but as I was advancing and getting closer it opened, I entered it. It was empty and intact as before. I went to a corner of the cave, where Mother Emperor was standing on the last day. I felt their presence one by one. Until the emperor came to me, I asked her to speak to him outside the cave, and he accepted. It was not easy to focus on a particular topic in a crowd place where there are a large number of people of your own and different in sizes.

“I have come here to see you and hear the sentence you had said about the body and the soul once again.” I said to her.

“The body is the house of spirit and the soul is engaging in the design of the body and nobody feels unpleasant at home. “She answered. I was surprised that the sentence was still clearly remembered. We, Emperors, have a great difference with you, humans, in this case. The Emperors keep their spirits the same and try to change their bodies to find the most suitable home for it, which is hard. While you humans try your best to keep your body constant and expose your spirits in thunders of events. Changing of spirit does not matter to you. The spirit of all of you, human, is same at birth, but your body has been created from birth to death. You will then change your soul through your deeds. Then, you will continue to make these changes so that you will end up in the habit. Not knowing, changing a habit is not so easy. Indeed, why do you change your spirit? Why are you trying to change your unwritten tablet? What is wrong with the original blankness?” She said.

“Unwritten plaque, you said? How do we change this unwritten plaque?" I asked her.

“It's much easier than you thought. Using your work, you are unaware that the result of your actions will be recorded in the most protected part of the creation, which is, your soul! ” she said.

“Do the actions affect the soul?” I asked.

“Yes, surely, you do not feel this change?" she answered.

I asked her to explain more about this. What do you mean by not feeling this change? "Each action that you perform for the first time has an effect on your soul. If you enjoyed it, your work was good and consistent with your nature. Because your spirit will be cuddled for your recording. But if you feel bad doing it, you know your action is bad and inconsistent with your nature. So your soul carries it feeling pain. "

"The pain from the wound will disappear after a while, but the mental discomfort will remain until the end of life." I asked.

"Do not you remember if your wound got off when you see the remaining effect?" she answered.

"Yes." I answered.

"Your soul is the same way, it feels bitter every time it comes to the effect of your work!" she continued.

"How affects the good deeds the human soul?" I asked her.

"Like exercising for the body, do not forget your soul is not from the material at all. So, you cannot clean out the effects of bad and good work, and only their effect will be diminished. "She said.

After that, she asked me to end this conversation. We went back into the cave with each other. All the creatures that had come to the cave at that time were gathered together, and there was a hunch between them. "The Savior comes."

Almost the only place I could stand was in the middle of the cave. But this time, I had a pleasant sense for all of them! Even though I had no intention of staying in that cave, I stayed at night and pass all that night in conversation. I told the Hunters of the intruders of that park, and they also said they would be happy to eat a few evil villagers. They also said some of their own work. In the morning, every group went to their own place, I was the last to leave the cave walking toward the city. On the way to the road, an old car stopped for me and I returned to town with him. I went to the airport waiting for the first flight to our new city. Went straight to our house from the airport. My mind was constantly busy. I thought of what happened in the last few days. My parents also noticed this change in my behavior. My mother wanted to ask me some questions that my dad took her hand and told; "It's better to let him be alone... " I went to the porch in front of the house sitting on one of the chairs, looking at the view across the house. The watercourse was bright in front of the house, and the glow of the sun's rays was magnificent. The next few days spent most of my time walking in the garden. Although the company's second project started, I asked for a few days to start my work with a delay of a few days. I summarized the results of the experiment and the conversations I had with the marker, I had been talking a little over the past few days, seeing my parents worry about my work with concern and distantly. Despite their great concern, they were respecting my privacy. The questions I should answer at this stage ordered within several floors.

"Does the human soul have a material state?" the first question.

The result of all these studies was a material state for the human soul can be considered in no way. The Mother Emperor said humans are born with the same spirit, such as the white tablet. Perhaps this sentence was consistent with the notion that every human being was born at the time of the birth innocent, but what was meant by the same spirit?

In my studies, I had been able to measure the amount of newborn babies weighing before death. This was separated from those who were officially weighing their weight in the care unit. I did this through the neonatal unit. That was interestingly to see, the weight deducted from all those babies was almost the same. Perhaps, as the Mother Emperor said; "Human actions affect its soul and cause its development through spirituality or its weakening due to sins. Therefore, the human soul changes throughout his life, apart from his body, but the soul is influenced by his actions. " Therefore, the human spirit and body, although separate, are in close contact with each other. Finally, human actions affect its weight. But, the question was still exist; how could it be possible, even though the human soul did not have a material state, but with a man's death and an outflow of spirit from his body, his weight changed very little?

I first read the article to find the answer to this question. Everyone knows that the two material bodies force each other, which is called the force of gravity. Obviously, body weight is affected by gravity. Considering this fact, each material with equal mass in different places of the universe has different weights. Hence, maybe these changes will affect its character! Now, I remembered the sentence of the injured man who said; "He felt a tensile force made him unable to move on." Therefore, there may be a similar force to the gravitational force between the two material are exist between the human soul and the body. From the words of the wounded who came back to life, it was concluded this force had the same gravity force and lowered it down. Therefore, the greatest impact of this force on Earth has been on human souls. Finally, it can be concluded, in addition to the gravitational force between the two materials, there is also a gravitational force between the material and the human soul. There will inevitably be a gravitational force between matter and non-matter, which is a gravitational force of a different kind. This is the same force that exists between man's matter and soul! Therefore, there must be a gravitational force between two non-materials which is most likely to be seen in the spirit of human beings. When two people see each other for the first time, they may have an inner attraction, while they have similar spirits. In this case, these people will feel good about each other. If these people have different spirits, they feel repulsive in themselves, in which case these people are not feeling well with each other, and they will feel no wanting toward each other. However, I heard somewhere that two different people, if they were traveling together and communicating with each other for a while, their morals and mood would be similar. It can be said this also happens debt to this fact that the stronger soul will attract the weaker soul! Perhaps the reason for the weight loss of the human body after death is this fact that the force existed between the human soul and the earth (dependence). After death, the human soul is no longer in the human body due to separation and independence, this force will be applied to its soul in a place other than the human body. The force that comes from the earth to the human body is reduced, so we must consider two weights for any substance that has the spirit: The first is the weight of its existing body, and the second is the weight of its soul, which, can be considered as a weighty one due to its insignificant weight. This issue can be verified as can be seen in physical relationships. The most interesting thing is that the properties of the material with the non-material relationship will be photographed.

For example, two substances repel each other with their equivalents, while two non-substances of the same nature absorb each other; two good people absorb each other. Another point in this experiment was considerable, where was the position of the soul in which part of the human body? It can be argued that if the human soul is separated of matter, it can flow without any problems everywhere in the human body and, in so many cases, manages and controls the entire human body until the relationship between the human soul and the human body is not interrupted. If there was a special place in the body for the soul, doctors and anatomists and surgeons had found it so far. So the soul is wide of all human bodies, if it is concentrated in somewhere, was not expected. While human mass fully matures its weight. Therefore, the weight of the soul in the whole human body is widespread, and it can also be said that what is known as weight loss in humans before death and after death is in fact a force or a heavy burden of matter! The relationship between gravity and matter and non-material matter also exist is considered as another reason for the unity of the human soul from its body, which happen due this fact that; Any material can pass through the material, resulting in different penetration times based on the penetration coefficient of the material between the two materials. So, if we want to pass a material from another matter at a shorter time than it determines the penetration coefficient of matter in its relationship, it will either leave the article or two unwittingly in effect. It's like passing a bullet from a watermelon that is caused by the passage of a material from another material at high speed, causing the watermelon to burst, and its structural disintegration. To justify the extent of the effect of the passage of matter on another substance, there is a formula and a coefficient of effect on the substance, and the duration of the passage of matter from each other affects it, which determines the amount of effect or perhaps unwanted effect on the material. Therefore, if the human soul had a material state occurs according to these formulas and coefficients when leaving the human body in the short time that death, it would have its effect or result, and we are able to see the effect of the exodus of the soul from the human body from the works. Based on these coefficients and formulas it can be concluded the human soul is single of matter and has a separate nature. In addition, along with this soul, there is the effects of human actions.

Chapter IX
Vacation

The high pressure of the work I did during this period made me feel tired. So, I went to a coastal town to spend a good holiday there suggested of my family. Certainly the peace I could find on the seashore could not be found elsewhere. I was sitting on the beach and looking at the people who crossed. So

me of them quickly jumped in the water, and others were slowly leaving the water. Suddenly, I thought of the penetration coefficient of matter and its relations and its related formulas. What would be useful to think about? We could create new materials using these relationships, formulas and coefficients, which are called Meta materials. We could create different species of these materials. So that they quickly change their penetration rate, and once they pass through a material; their diffusion coefficient varies having another penetration factor and affects another. I got up from my place and started walking on the beach sand to get rid of these scientific issues. It was really fascinating. A few boys were playing in front of me, while threw balloons thrown around each other. One of them was running in front of me and his friend threw a balloon full of water at his side.

The boy took a small box filled with water-filled balloons in front of his face. I saw the balloon traversing a semicircular path to the boy's box in front of me, and the contents of the water spread to me on my face and my body and part of my clothes poured, the boy looked at me and said: "sorry."

I asked the boy to come closer: "What is inside the balloons?"

"Water." The boy replied.

"How many of these balloons do you have?" I said.

"Two or three boxes like this, but I must wet them with my friends standing there." I asked.

"Lonely?" I said.

"Yes" he said.

"Do not you want to check with one another?" I asked the little boy.

"I want, but who?" he said.

A few seconds later, I was running along with that boy and followed his friends and gave them a balloon full of water. I thought I had soaked them with water-filled balloons, but by looking at myself, I noticed that there was not even a single point of my clothes!

When playing water with that boy, the kids got rid of the thoughts that I've always been involved with. However, it was too late and I had to return to my place of residence. I said goodbye to that guy and asked one of them: "Will you come to the lips of tomorrow?"

"Of course I'm coming." I said.

Tomorrow morning, I noticed that the three boys and two others killed me with six boxes of water-filled balloons and six spray guns, so I went ahead and asked them: "What do you do here?"

"Waiting for you, why are you late?" They said. They drove me on the beach to come and play with each other, they even brought me a sprinkler gun and a box of water-filled balloons. I was very happy about this, and I said to myself, I wish everyone was behaving like these guys. I was so excited about the quality of the kids, so we went to one of the sure lines of the sea to buy our own camera and some other devices, and so our group was ready to play water. One of the tools at the store was a device that could use air pressure to throw balloons full of water at a distance. It was interesting to see there were several set levers to determine where to throw the balloons. We had the toy hats keeping wireless toys. Every man guarded one person and the rest were building a sand castle. In the afternoon, we had two sand castles on the beach, the two groups were throwing balloons full of water together and setting up the device to throw balloons full of water toward each other. After the filled water balloons finished, each group was attacked with spray guns, and soaked up as much as we could. At the end, we were standing in the water and looking at the sea. Some of people on the beach were looking at me and they were excited to see me playing with a few boys, and they were dating together for the water playing. We spent the rest of the day along with those boys on the beach lane and plotted for our sand castle tomorrow. In the morning, I had to go to the coast earlier than usual to join the boys. When we came along with those boys from the place we were set up to play together, we saw a marvelous scene. A large number of people were not only building sand castles, but also they brought plenty of water jets and water-filled balloons.

"Today, we must all stay together so that we can overcome this!" I said. At the corner of the beach, which was closed from behind, and no one could get wet from there, we began to build our castle. I looked at the castles and trenches of the rest of the people on the beach, some of which represented a great art of their builders. A person was walking through the castles with a box in his hand, giving each a flag, it was supposed that every castle with more flags would win this coastal competition. As the competition started, I and those five boys were well versed and I think it was due to our practice of yesterday. In addition to balloons filled with water and spray guns, we also had a device that, threw water balloons into other castles, and this was our advantage on the first day and our superiority. The next day, as I was leaving that city, I crossed the coast and seeing that our next castle, which was wetted by us yesterday, has four ballistic devices full of water and is busy wetting other groups. One of those castles, closed two of these devices on a plate and simultaneously threw two balloons into other groups in an innovative work...

www.ingramcontent.com/pod-product-compliance
Ingram Content Group UK Ltd.
Pitfield, Milton Keynes, MK11 3LW, UK
UKHW020239250726
13967UKWH00001B/456

9 781387 943586